W9-BTJ-592

I ♥ DINOSAURS®

FLYING DINOSAURS
Pterodactyls

Written and illustrated by
Michael Berenstain

A GOLDEN BOOK • NEW YORK
Western Publishing Company, Inc., Racine, Wisconsin 53404

Long ago, reptiles ruled the Earth.

There were many different kinds of reptiles. There were crocodiles, turtles, lizards and snakes, much like those you see today. But there were other, stranger kinds as well.

On the land, the giant dinosaurs were king.

In the sea, great sea serpent–shaped reptiles ruled the waves.

But in the air—who ruled the skies?

The skies of long ago were ruled by the pterosaurs (TER-o-saurs). Their name means "winged lizard," and that is just how they looked.

Their wings were made of skin stretched over bony "fingers." One family was called the pterodactyls (ter-o-DAC-tles)— "winged fingers."

Most pterodactyls were about the size of sea gulls. They may have lived like sea birds, too—flying along the shore catching fish or other small sea creatures.

Pterodactyl wings were long and narrow, similar to those of birds. But, like bats, their wings had claws.

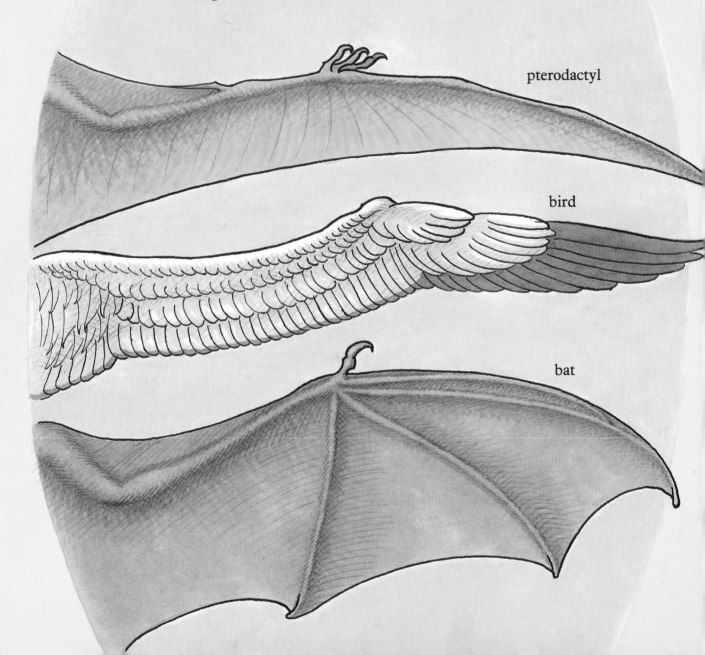

pterodactyl

bird

bat

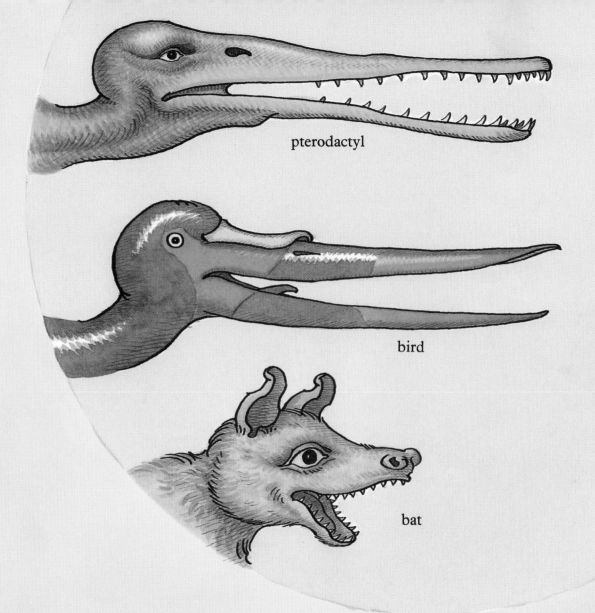

pterodactyl

bird

bat

Pterodactyl beaks were also long and narrow,
like most birds'. But, again like bats, they
usually had many sharp teeth.

One of the larger pterosaurs was Pteranodon (ter-AH-no-don). It had a wingspan of twenty-four feet. It was one of the few pterosaurs that had no teeth. Its name means "winged no-tooth."

Pteranodon may have lived like a modern pelican—catching fish in the sea and carrying them back to its nest in a large throat pouch.

Its nest may have been built on high sea cliffs to protect its helpless young from meat-eating dinosaurs.

Pteranodon had a high crest on its head. This may have helped to balance its long beak. Different kinds of Pteranodons had differently shaped crests.

Pteranodon ingens
(ter-AH-no-don IN-gens)

crest

crest

Pteranodon sternbergia
(ter-AH-no-don stern-BERG-ia)

Pteranodon

Though Pteranodon was big, it was not the biggest pterosaur of all. Even bigger was Quetzalcoatlus (quet-zal-co-AHT-lus). This flying giant had a wingspan of forty feet—the size of a small airplane!

Quetzalcoatlus

Quetzalcoatlus did not live near the sea like
most pterosaurs. It lived far inland. It may have
caught fish in rivers or lakes. Or it might have
been a vulture-like scavenger that fed on the
carcasses of dead dinosaurs.

Most pterosaurs were much, much smaller than Quetzalcoatlus. The smallest of all was Pterodactylus elegans—"elegant winged finger." It was not much bigger than a robin.

Quetzalcoatlus

robin

Pterodactylus elegans

Dimorphodon
(di-MORF-o-don)

Like the birds of today, different kinds of
pterosaurs had differently shaped beaks.
Dimorphodon had a big toucan-like bill that
may have been brightly colored to attract a
mate.

One strange pterosaur had a long, curving beak full of fine hairlike teeth. It probably used them to strain the tiny creatures it ate from muddy water.

Pterodaustro
(ter-o-DAUS-tro)

Dsungaripterus
(jung-a-RIP-ter-us)

Another pterosaur had a pointed upturned beak. It may have been used to pry open oysters and clams.

The first pterosaurs were different from their later pterodactyl relatives. They were all small- or medium-sized, with shorter beaks full of teeth. Most had long tails—some with flaps on the end. These helped them to steer in flight.

Rhamphorhynchus
(ram-fo-RINK-us)

One early pterosaur may have had fur on its body. A fossil from Russia seems to show a thick, hairy pelt. This may be the only reptile fossil ever found showing fur.

Sordes
(SOR-deez)

A small, short-tailed early pterosaur had a blunt beak with peglike teeth. Scientists think it ate insects, catching them in flight like a bat.

Anurognathus
(a-noor-og-NATH-us)

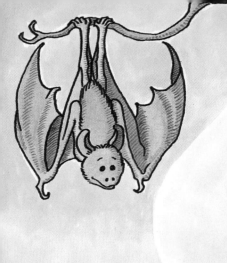

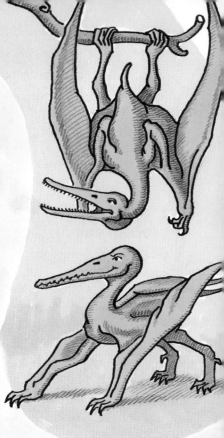

For years, scientists have puzzled over how pterosaurs stood and walked. Since these creatures had batlike wings and claws, most scientists thought they must have lived like bats, too—hanging from branches or cliffs, and crawling on the ground.

bats

pterosaurs

today's bird

But, now, many scientists think that pterosaurs folded their wings across their backs and walked on their hind legs, like birds.

Though pterosaurs looked like bats and birds, they were not closely related to either.

A few scientists think that pterosaurs were true dinosaurs. Others believe they were dinosaur cousins.

This family tree shows how most scientists think they evolved.

Birds were probably an offshoot of the dinosaur family.

Pterosaurs may have come from the same reptile ancestors as the dinosaurs themselves.

Bats probably came from early mammals that looked like mice.

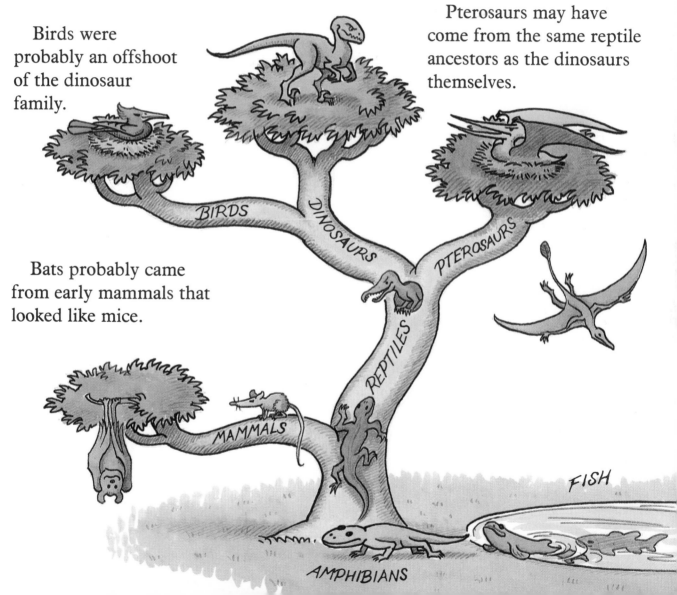

BIRDS

DINOSAURS

PTEROSAURS

REPTILES

MAMMALS

FISH

AMPHIBIANS

The first true bird lived at about the same time as the early pterosaurs. Its name, Archaeopteryx (ark-ee-OP-ter-ix), means "old wing."

It looked like a mixture of reptile and bird. It had feathers like a bird, but teeth, claws, and a long tailbone like a reptile.

It was about the size of a crow.

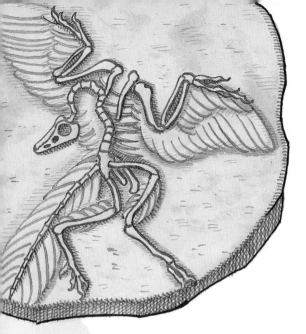

We know this early bird had feathers, from the fine quality of the fossils that have been found in Germany.

Earlier, when the first pterosaur fossils were found in the same place, some scientists thought they were sea creatures. Their wings were mistaken for flippers!

The large fossil skeletons of
Pteranodons were discovered in Kansas
in the Wild West days of the 1870's.

Scientists brought the fossils back East, reconstructed the skeletons, and hung them in their museums. We can see them there today—soaring overhead—and imagine how they looked in the skies of long ago.

Pterosaurs died out at the same time as their dinosaur cousins.

But birds, dinosaur grandchildren, lived on. Why?

No one knows.

Perhaps, one day, the secret will be discovered. Perhaps *you* will be the ones to find out.